yummy

Eight Favorite Fairy Tales

For Jo

First U.S. edition 2009

Library of Congress Cataloging-in-Publication Data is available.

Library of Congress Catalog Card Number 2008938763

ISBN 978-0-7636-4474-1

09 10 11 12 13 14 CCP 10 9 8 7 6 5 4 3

Printed in Shenzhen, Guangdong, China

This book was typeset in Gill Sans MT Schoolbook
with hand lettering by the author-illustrator.
The illustrations were done in gouache.

Candlewick Press
99 Dover Street
Somerville, Massachusetts 02144

www.candlewick.com

yummy

Eight Favorite Fairy Tales

Lucy Cousins

CANDLEWICK PRESS

Contents

Little Red Riding

Once upon a time, there was
a girl named Little Red Riding Hood.
Her mother asked her to take a
basket of food through the woods
to her grandmother, who was ill.

Hood

11

Little Red Riding Hood had not gone
far when she met a wolf.
"Where are you going, Little Red
Riding Hood?" the wolf asked.
"I am taking a basket of food to
my grandmother, because she is ill,"
answered Little Red Riding Hood.
"Is that so?" said the wolf with a
nasty grin, and away he ran.

13

The wolf ran straight to Grandmother's

house and knocked at the door.

"Who's there?" called Grandmother.

"It's me, Little Red Riding Hood," said

the wolf in a sweet little voice. "I've

brought you a basket of food."

"Come in then," said Grandmother.

gulp!

The wolf went in, leaped onto
Grandmother's bed, and
swallowed her whole.

17

After a while, Little Red Riding Hood arrived.

She walked into the house and went over to the bed.

"Grandmother, what big eyes you have," she said.

"All the better to see you with, my dear," replied the wolf.

"Grandmother, what big ears you have."

"All the better to hear you with, my dear."

"Grandmother, what big teeth you have."

"All the better to *eat* you with, my dear!"

And with that the wolf leaped out of bed
and gobbled up Little Red Riding Hood.

A hunter was passing by and heard
the noise. He came in and
saw the wicked wolf.

chop!

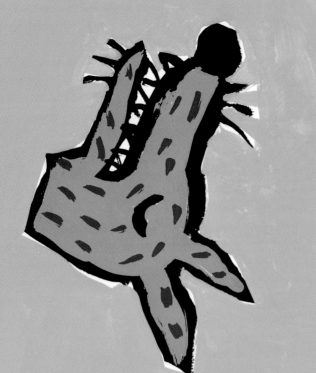

He chopped the wolf open,
and out stepped Grandmother
and Little Red Riding Hood.
"HOORAY!" they cried.
Then they ate up the food
in the basket and lived
happily ever after.

The Three

Billy Goats Gruff

Once upon a time, there were three billy goats: Big Billy Goat Gruff, Middle Billy Goat Gruff, and Little Billy Goat Gruff. They lived on a hillside by a river. The grass on the far side of the river looked so green that one day they decided to go and eat it. But first they had to cross the bridge, and under the bridge lived a great ugly troll.

First Little Billy Goat Gruff stepped onto
the bridge. *Trip-trap, trip-trap* went his hooves.
"Who's that tripping over my bridge?"
roared the troll.
"It's me," said Little Billy Goat Gruff in
a very little voice.
"I'm going to gobble you up," said the troll.
"Oh please don't eat me," said Little Billy
Goat Gruff. "I'm only small. Wait for the
next billy goat. He's much bigger."
"Well, be off with you,"
said the troll.

Trip-trap

25

Then Middle Billy Goat Gruff stepped onto the bridge.

Trip-trap, trip-trap went his hooves.

"Who's that trip-trapping over my bridge?"

roared the troll.

"It's me," said Middle Billy Goat Gruff in a middle-size voice.

"I'm going to gobble you up,"

said the troll.

"Oh, please don't

eat me," said

Middle Billy Goat

Gruff. "I'm only middle-size.

Wait for the next billy

goat. He's much bigger."

"Well, be off with you,"

said the troll.

Trip-
trap

27

Trip-trap

Big Billy Goat Gruff stepped onto

the bridge. *Trip-trap, trip-trap*

went his hooves very loudly.

"Who's that stomping over my

bridge?" roared the troll.

"It's me," said Big Billy Goat Gruff

in his great big voice.

"I'm going to gobble you up,"

said the troll.

"Then I'll bash you to bits,"

said Big Billy Goat Gruff.

29

Big Billy Goat Gruff put his head down and charged at the troll, butting him so hard that he flew up into the air and then down into the middle of the river.

The troll was never seen again, and the billy goats got so fat eating grass on the far side of the river that they were scarcely able to walk home again.

The Enormous Turnip

Once upon a time, an old man
wanted to grow turnips, so he scattered
some seeds in his garden and said,
"Grow, seeds, grow. Grow into big
juicy turnips."

He pulled and

The next morning the old man
went out to the garden and
found that one enormous
turnip had grown. But when
he tried to pull it up, he
pulled and he pulled but
it wouldn't come out.

34

he pulled.

The old man called an old woman.

"Please help me pull up the turnip," he said.

The old woman called a boy.

"Please help us pull up the turnip," she said.

The boy called a girl.

"Please help us pull up the turnip," he said.

They pulled and

They pulled and they pulled but the enormous turnip just wouldn't come out.

they pulled.

"Dog, Dog, help us pull up the turnip," called the girl.

They pulled and they pulled.

"Cat, Cat, help us pull up the turnip," called the dog.

They pulled and they pulled.

"Mouse, Mouse, help us pull up the turnip," called the cat.

They pulled and they pulled and they pulled . . .

They pulled and they pulled . . .

and at last out came the turnip!

They took the turnip
home and chopped it
and cooked it and had

an enormous feast—
and they are probably
still eating it now!

43

Henny Penny

Once upon a time, an acorn fell on Henny Penny's head. "Oh, dear!" said Henny Penny. "The sky is falling. I must go and tell the king."

She went along, and she went along, and soon she met Cocky Locky.

"Where are you going?" asked Cocky Locky.

"I'm going to tell the king that the sky is falling," said Henny Penny.

"May I come with you?" asked Cocky Locky.

"Certainly," said Henny Penny.

They went along, and they went along, and soon
they met Ducky Daddles.

"Where are you going?" asked Ducky Daddles.

"We're going to tell the king that the sky is falling,"
said Henny Penny and Cocky Locky.

"May I come with you?" asked Ducky Daddles.

"Certainly," said the others.

They went along

They went along, and they went along, and soon

they met Goosey Poosey.

"Where are you going?" asked Goosey Poosey.

"We're going to tell the king that the sky is falling,"

said Henny Penny, Cocky Locky,

and Ducky Daddles.

and they went along.

"May I come with you?"

asked Goosey Poosey.

"Certainly," said the others.

They went along, and they went along, and soon

they met Turkey Lurkey.

"Where are you going?" asked Turkey Lurkey.

"We're going to tell the king that the sky is falling,"

said Henny Penny, Cocky Locky,

Ducky Daddles, and Goosey Poosey.

"May I come with you?"
asked Turkey Lurkey.

"Certainly," said the others.

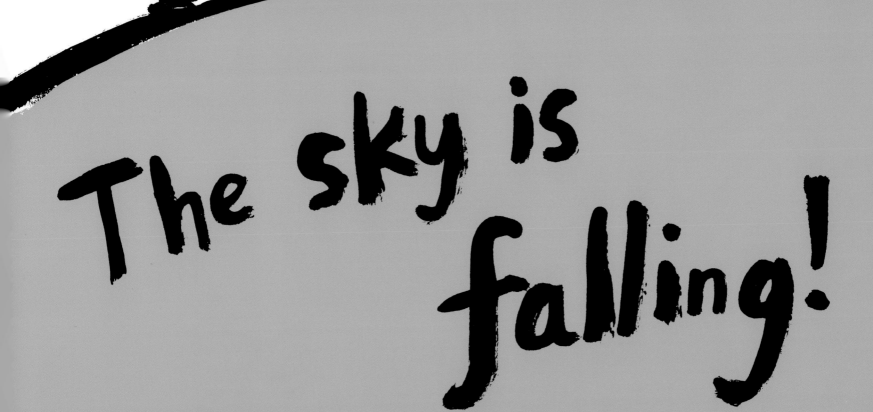

The sky is
falling!

Soon they met Foxy Woxy.

50

They went along, and they went along, and soon

they met Foxy Woxy.

"Where are you going?" asked Foxy Woxy.

"We're going to tell the king that the sky is falling,"

said Henny Penny, Cocky Locky, Ducky Daddles,

Goosey Poosey, and Turkey Lurkey.

"But this is not the way to the king,"

said Foxy Woxy. "Let me show

you the way."

"Thank you," they said.

This is the way.

Foxy Woxy led them to a dark and narrow hole.

"This is the way to the king," he said. "I'll go

first, and you follow."

"Why of course! Certainly! Without doubt! Why not?"

said Henny Penny, Cocky Locky, Ducky Daddles,

Goosey Poosey, and Turkey Lurkey.

Turkey Lurkey went into the hole first.

CRUNCH! MUNCH!

Foxy Woxy gobbled up Turkey Lurkey.

hee hee hee

Goosey Poosey went into the hole next.

CRUNCH! MUNCH!

Foxy Woxy gobbled up Goosey Poosey.

Ducky Daddles went into the hole next.

CRUNCH! MUNCH!

Foxy Woxy gobbled
up Ducky Daddles.

Cocky Locky
went into the
hole next.

CRUNCH! — Foxy Woxy
tried to gobble up Cocky Locky
but missed.

"Oh, help!" cried Cocky Locky.

CRUNCH! MUNCH! Foxy Woxy *did* gobble up Cocky Locky.

56

Oh, help!

Henny Penny heard Cocky Locky, and she turned and ran home as fast as she could. So she never did tell the king that the sky was falling.

Goldilocks and

Once upon a time, there were three bears—

Papa Bear, Mama Bear, and Baby Bear.

They lived in a cottage in the woods. Every morning

they made porridge for breakfast—a big bowl

for Papa Bear, a medium-size bowl for

Mama Bear, and a little bowl for Baby Bear.

One morning, the porridge was very hot.

"Let's go for a walk while it cools down,"

Mama Bear said. And off they went.

the Three Bears

While the three bears were out, a

little girl named Goldilocks came to

the cottage and went straight inside.

"Oh, look! Lovely porridge!" she said.

She was very hungry.

First she tried the porridge in the big bowl.

"Too hot," she said.

Then she tried the porridge in the

medium-size bowl.

"Too salty," she said.

Yummy

Then she tried
the porridge in
the little bowl.
"Just right,"
she said, and
ate it all up.

"Now I will try one of these chairs," said Goldilocks.

First she tried the big chair.

"Too hard," she said.

Then she tried the

medium-size chair.

"Too soft," she said.

Crash!

Then she tried the little chair.

"Just right," she said,

but when she sat on it—

CRACK! CRASH!

it broke into pieces.

Goldilocks was tired and wanted to
lie down, so she went upstairs.
First she tried the big bed.
"Too high," she said.
Next she tried the
medium-size bed.
"Too lumpy," she said.

64

Then she tried the little bed.

"Just right," she said,

and soon fell fast asleep.

ZZzzzZZZZ Z...

Someone's been

eating my porridge.

Before long, the

three bears came home.

They looked at their bowls.

"Someone's been eating my porridge,"

said Papa Bear.

"And someone's been eating *my* porridge,"

said Mama Bear.

"And someone's been eating *my* porridge, and

it's all gone," said Baby Bear.

Then the three bears looked at their chairs.

"Someone's been sitting in my chair," said Papa Bear.

"And someone's been sitting in *my* chair," said Mama Bear.

"And someone's been sitting in *my* chair, and now it's broken to pieces," said Baby Bear.

Someone's been sitting in my chair.

Someone's been lying in my bed.

70

Then the three bears went upstairs.

"Someone's been lying in my bed,"

said Papa Bear.

"And someone's been lying in

my bed," said Mama Bear.

"And someone's been lying in
my bed," said Baby Bear.
"Look, there she is!"

Look,

When Goldilocks woke up and saw the three bears, she jumped out of bed and leaped out of the window and ran and ran away from the cottage.

The three bears never saw her again.

75

The Little Red Hen

Once upon a time,
there was a little red hen
who lived with a dog,
a goose, and a cat.
One day the
little red hen
found some
grains of wheat.
"Who will help me plant
this wheat?" she asked.

"I'm busy," said the dog.

"I'm busy," said the goose.

"I'm busy," said the cat.

"Then I shall plant it myself," said the little red hen.

And she did.

Every day the little red hen watered and
weeded the ground, until tiny shoots appeared.
Slowly the shoots grew tall and strong.
Then one day the wheat was ready for cutting.

I'm busy.

"Who will help me cut the wheat?" asked the little red hen.

I'm busy.

"I'm busy," said the dog.

"I'm busy," said the goose.

"I'm busy," said the cat.

"Then I shall cut it myself,"

said the little red hen.

And she did.

I'm busy.

Soon the wheat was ready to be taken to the mill

to be ground into flour.

"Who will help me take the wheat to the mill?"

asked the little red hen.

"I'm busy," said the dog.

"I'm busy," said the goose.

"I'm busy," said the cat.

"Then I'll take it myself," said the little red hen. And she did.

She took the wheat

to the mill.

83

She baked the bread.

The little red hen brought the flour back home.

Now it was time for baking.

"Who will help me bake the bread?"

asked the little red hen.

"I'm busy," said the dog.

"I'm busy," said the goose.

"I'm busy," said the cat.

"Then I'll bake it myself,"

said the little red hen.

And she did.

When the little red hen took the bread
out of the oven, it smelled delicious.

"Who will help me eat the bread?"

asked the little red hen.

"I will," said the dog.

"I will," said the goose.

"I will," said the cat.

"Oh, no, you won't," said the little red hen,

and she ate it all up herself.

Oh, no, you won't.

The

Three Little Pigs

Once upon a time, there was a
mother pig with three little pigs. They
were so poor that the mother pig sent
the little pigs away to seek their fortunes.

The first little pig
met a man with a
bundle of straw.
"Please, sir," said the little
pig, "give me that straw
to build a house."
The man did, and the
little pig built his house.

Please, sir.

Then along came a wolf, who knocked at the door.

"Little Pig, Little Pig," the wolf called, "let me come in."

The little pig answered, "Not by the hair

of my chinny-chin-chin!"

So the wolf said,

"Then I'll huff and I'll puff, and

I'll blow your house in!"

Let me
Come in.

And he huffed and
he puffed, and he
blew the house in
and ate up the
first little pig.

93

The second little pig met a man
with a bundle of sticks.

Please, sir.

"Please, sir," said the little pig,
"give me those sticks to build a house."
The man did, and the little
pig built his house.

Then along came the wolf, who knocked at the door.

"Little Pig, Little Pig", the wolf called, "let me come in."

The little pig answered,

"Not by the hair of my chinny-chin-chin!"

So the wolf said,

"Then I'll huff and I'll puff,

and I'll blow your house in!"

And he huffed and
he puffed, and he blew
the house in and ate up
the second little pig.

The third little pig met a man
with a load of bricks.
"Please, sir," he said,
"give me those bricks
to build a house."
The man did,
and the little pig
built his house.

Please, sir.

huff, puff!

Then along came the wolf,

who knocked at the door.

"Little Pig, Little Pig," the

wolf called, "let me come in."

The little pig answered,

"Not by the hair of

my chinny-chin-chin!"

So the wolf said,

"Then I'll huff and I'll puff,

and I'll blow your house in!"

And he huffed and he puffed,

but he could not blow

the house in.

101

The wolf was very angry.

"Little Pig," he said, "I'm going to climb down your chimney and eat you up!"

So the little pig made a blazing fire and put a huge pot of water on to boil.

grrrr

As the wolf was coming down the chimney, the little pig took the lid off the pot, and the wolf fell in. The little pig put the lid back on and boiled up the wolf and ate him for supper.

The little pig lived happily ever after.

Bye-bye, Wolf.

105

106

The Musicians of Bremen

Once upon a time, a donkey decided to go to Bremen to become a musician. On the way, he met a sad dog. "What is the matter, Dog?" asked the donkey. "Nobody loves me," said the dog. "Come with me to Bremen and be a musician," said the donkey. "I'll play the guitar, and you can play the drums." So they went together down the road.

Soon they met a sad cat.
"What is the matter, Cat?"
asked the donkey.
"Nobody loves me,"
said the cat.
"Come with us to Bremen
and be a musician,"
said the donkey. "I'll play
the guitar, Dog will play
the drums, and you can
play the violin."
So they went together
down the road.

What is

the matter?

Soon they met a sad rooster.

"What is the matter, Rooster?" asked the donkey.

"Nobody loves me," said the rooster.

"Come with us to Bremen and be a musician," said the donkey.

"I'll play the guitar, Dog will play the drums, Cat will

play the violin, and you can sing."

So they went down the

road until nightfall.

In the dark, they came across a robbers' house.

Donkey peeped in through a window.

"What can you see?" asked Dog, Cat, and Rooster.

"Lots of food and a warm fire," said Donkey.

"What else?" asked the others.

"Four robbers eating their dinner," said Donkey.

The animals made a plan to chase out the robbers.
Donkey stood with his hooves against the window.
Dog stood on Donkey's back, Cat on Dog's back, and
Rooster on Cat's head. Then they made music.
Hee-haw! Woof, woof! Meow! Cock-a-doodle-doo!
And they fell through the window with a mighty crash!

The robbers were so
frightened that they
ran away.

Donkey, Dog, Cat, and
Rooster ate all the food.
Then they went to bed.

Donkey found some straw outside in the yard.

Dog lay down behind the door.

Cat curled up by the fire.

Rooster flew up onto the roof.

Soon they were fast asleep.

During the night, one of the robbers crept back into the cottage. He tried to light a match from the embers of the fire. But the embers were Cat's eyes, and she leaped at him, hissing and scratching. He stepped back onto Dog, who bit him in the leg. He ran into the yard, and Donkey kicked him. Then Rooster crowed, *Cock-a-doodle-doo!*

Help!

The robber ran back to his friends.

"There's a witch in the house who scratched

my face," he cried. "And there's a man with a knife who

stabbed me in the leg. And there's a monster in the yard

who beat me with a club. And there's a judge up above

who shouted, 'I'll lock you up, you rascal, you!'"

The robbers were so scared that they

never came back again.

120

And Donkey, Dog, Cat, and Rooster

never went to Bremen,

but lived happily ever after

in the cottage.